MARKED: MYRON

A FOSTER BROTHERS PREQUEL

NORA PHOENIX

Love,

Nora

MARKED: MYRON

A crazy bet has tattoo legend Abel offering his big, hairy ass to the one man he can't get out of his head: newcomer Myron.

For a tattoo, though anything else is definitely on the table as well.

Half his age and size and bossy as can be, Myron should not be Abel's type, if only because he's a man and Abel has always thought he was straight. Yeah, not so much. Myron has gotten under his skin, and now Abel wants him on his skin as well...and in his life.

What starts as a drunken bet becomes a scorching hot encounter. Myron makes it clear that's all he wants, but Abel needs more. He'll do whatever it takes to tame Myron, even if it means letting Myron be on top of things...

THE FOSTER BROTHERS

Marked is a prequel to a new contemporary MM romance series called *The Foster Brothers*.

Jaren, Hadley, Lagan, and Nordin chose to be brothers after growing up in foster care together, and now nothing can come between them...not even when they find love.

Jilted - Jaren: could it be that getting dumped the day before his wedding and taken in by his ex-fiancée's brother is the best thing that could've ever happened to Jaren?

Hired - Hadley: Hadley makes the mistake of falling for the worst guy possible: his grumpy billionaire boss

Loathed - Lagan: When mutual hate between Lagan and his law professor turns into something else entirely...

Nicked - Nordin: The stupidest thing a con artist can ever do is fall for the man who's trying to catch him...

1

What had he done?

Abel DiRossi stared at the intricate, colorful letters on the window from a safe distance, not wanting to run the risk that Myron would spot him. *Rainbow Ink.* The tattoo shop looked innocent enough, but Abel knew what danger lurked behind those windows and bright red doors.

He groaned. What the hell had he been thinking, making a bet with the one man who had him all in knots every time they met? And not only laying a wager but *losing* it, on purpose, and that while the stakes had been high.

He hadn't been thinking, which was the whole problem. Copious amounts of alcohol had clouded his brain and his judgment. He'd needed a few stiff drinks to be able to deal with Myron, since the man was too goddamn cocky and way too beautiful to endure sober, but that decision had proven to be a costly mistake.

He'd been desperate for his attention, so desperate he'd come up with this cockamamie plan on the fly after they'd run into each other in a bar, both of them out with friends.

If Abel had kept his wits about him, if he'd made the much smarter decision to stop drinking after the first three whiskeys, he wouldn't have been foolish enough to put up the most precious thing he had in a bet.

His ass.

As if Myron would simply swoon at the sight of Abel's bare ass—though some of his gay friends had assured him it was spectacular, so trustworthy sources. But still. What the hell had he been thinking?

He was *so* fucked.

He straightened his shoulders. He was a man of his word, and no one would ever be able to accuse him of breaking a promise, least of all Myron Larsen. The man was arrogant as it was—and why Abel found that hot was beyond him—and Abel wouldn't provide him with any more ammunition to fuel the dislike Myron already had for him. He seemed to have taken an aversion to Abel from the moment they had met. No, he'd swallow his pride and offer his virgin ass like he had promised.

Chin high and chest tight, he walked over to the shop and entered without giving himself another chance to reconsider. The familiar sounds and smells of a tattoo shop greeted him. With five permanent booths and room for a sixth, Rainbow Ink was bigger than Dreams Ink, the shop Abel worked in. He and Juliette, the owner, were the only two artists there, and the two of them worked rarely at the same time. He liked it that way, always having been a loner.

The woman closest to the entrance shut off her needle. What was her name again, Mari? Abel had met her once at a tattoo convention years ago but wasn't sure if he remembered her name correctly. "Hi. Can I help you?"

"I have an appointment with Myron."

Appointment wasn't the right word, but he could hardly tell her he was here because he'd lost a fucking bet.

She raised an eyebrow. "You sure about that, honey?" Then she took a better look at him, and recognition dawned in her eyes. "You're Abel DiRossi."

"Yeah."

Seattle might be a big city, but it wasn't that big, and the tattoo world was a small one. Occasionally, they ran into each other, especially when both shops were considered among the best in the city.

"Would you perhaps be the reason Myron is in a pisser of a mood? He's been stomping around like an elephant this morning, nursing what looks like the hangover from hell."

At least he wasn't the only one who'd indulged in too much alcohol. A small consolation, but he would take it. "I can't say with certainty, but I'd estimate the odds are in my favor."

She winced. "In that case, god be with you. He's in the back, and you can walk right in."

He nodded at her, then stalked to the back of the shop, passing two more artists at work. He would've loved to watch what they were working on, but if he didn't face Myron now, he'd lose his resolve. As was always the case when he knew he'd see him again, nerves were flaring up all throughout his body, sending his whole system into a frenzy. What was it with this guy that he had such an effect on him?

A chair creaked, a thud as if a boot stomped on the floor, followed by a grunt. He tracked the noises into a break room where a large, rectangle table sat in the middle with three chairs on each side. Myron, all gorgeous, slim, tattooed five-foot-nine of him, was parked in one of them, a scowl on his stunning face. His boss and the owner of the shop, Reid Welz, sat opposite him, looking stern. Abel had met Reid several times over the years, and while technically competitors, they got along well.

Abel cleared his throat, and both men turned their heads toward him. "Hi," he said stupidly, but his brain wouldn't come up with anything else. Not uncommon, unfortunately. He wasn't a smooth conversationalist at the best of times, but Myron always managed to strike him mute. Half Abel's size, he shouldn't even have been remotely intimidating, but the man had a mouth on him that could cut a person to pieces.

"The bet is off," Myron grumbled at Abel. "So you can leave now."

"What do you mean it's off?"

Myron nicked his chin in Reid's direction. "Someone ratted me out to Reid, and the boss won't allow it. Some crap about you being drunk and not being able to consent."

Reid let out a long-suffering sigh. "For fuck's sake, Myron, we've been over this. We don't tattoo people who are drunk, high, or otherwise incapable of giving consent."

"He's sober now," Myron pointed out, indicating Abel in a sharp gesture.

Reid pushed his chair back. "You two can fight this out among yourselves. I don't have time for this bullshit. My sister is getting married tomorrow, and she just texted me she needs to see me urgently because apparently some shit is going down, so I'm out of here." He walked over to Abel. "Good to see you, Abel."

"You too. Congrats on your sister's wedding. Did she pick a good guy?"

Reid's expression changed. "The best. Jaren is..." Emotions flashed over his face, too quickly for Abel to interpret, but something more was at play here than he was aware of. "He's great."

"Have fun at the wedding."

"Not fucking likely," Reid mumbled and then took off with a last fierce look in Myron's direction. What had that been about? Abel would have to worry about it later. He'd have his hands full with Myron.

Abel gingerly sat down on the chair Reid had vacated, meeting Myron's piercing blue eyes. He was so goddamn beautiful. The combination of his messy, dirty blond hair, that pale skin under the abundance of tattoos, and his slender, almost fragile body shouldn't even appeal to Abel. Hell, until he'd met Myron, he hadn't even been attracted to men. Myron was his exact opposite and a good ten years younger to boot. He was moody, cocky, and infuriating, and yet every time Abel saw him, he was speechless.

"So?" Myron scowled at him. "Are you gonna give me your ass or what?"

2

Myron had known Abel would show up. The man had too much honor and integrity not to, even if their bet had been a stupid one, fueled by too many drinks. Usually, Myron knew his limits and stopped after a few glasses, but Abel always made him drink more than he should. For some reason, the man pushed buttons inside Myron no one else did.

"I'm a man of my word," Abel said curtly.

Myron sighed. "Reid was right. You didn't voluntarily say yes to this."

"That must've pained you to admit."

"He's a reasonable guy, and he's strict on consent, which I happen to agree with."

"But as you rightfully pointed out, I'm sober now and able to give consent."

"Yeah, but you're one of those guys who has an honor complex, so even though you were drunk off your ass yesterday, making promises you probably can't even remember, you now feel obliged to honor your word."

The wince on Abel's face told Myron his words had hit the target. "You were just as drunk as me."

"True, but I'm not the one who lost the bet."

He didn't say that had been more luck than skill. He'd been so drunk he'd barely been able to see the cards in front of him and had no fucking clue how he'd managed to win. But he must've played his cards right because he had.

His memory of everything else was fine, however, and he remembered every detail of Abel's glorious body when he'd lost his shirt, then his pants. Stripped down to his underwear, he'd shown off most of his bear-sized body, which was covered from head to toe in tattoos, each of them more beautiful than the other, even slightly hidden behind the sexy fur he sported everywhere. He was exactly Myron's type...and also the kind of man Myron avoided at all costs.

Abel had gotten a good eyeful of Myron in his underwear as well, as their luck had gone back and forth. But he had probably not been as affected, seeing as he was straight. Their friends—though traitors was more apt as they'd done nothing to dissuade them from making some disastrous decisions—had egged them on to continue, whooping and cheering along with the crowd that had gathered around them every time one of them lost an article of clothing.

"So where does that leave us?" Abel asked, his brown eyes insecure.

Myron had always found it fascinating how such a big and imposing man could be so soft and almost endearing. He was full of confidence when he was tattooing. Myron had watched him at a demonstration once, and he hadn't been able to look away as Abel had free-drawn a bald eagle with incredibly detailed linework on a guy's back and then had inked it. But whenever they had interacted, Abel had lost some of that confidence and instead showed him a much softer side.

"It leaves you free to go. I won't hold you to your drunken bet."

Abel's mouth set in a stubborn line. "A promise is a promise, drunk or not."

Myron scoffed. "So if a client was drunk and said he wanted an *I love Mom* tattoo, you'd do it?"

"Of course not, but I knew what I was consenting to."

Myron raised an eyebrow. "You're telling me you willingly put up your virgin ass?"

Abel's cheeks reddened. "Yes. No? I don't know. I knew what I was doing is what I'm saying."

Something tickled in Myron's belly, that desire that always burned inside him whenever Abel was near. He'd never have him, of course. The idea of big, burly Abel giving up his ass to Myron was almost too ridiculous to consider. The man hadn't given any indication he wasn't straight, and even if by sheer luck he was bicurious, he'd never bend over for a twink. Men like him had expectations, and bottoming wasn't one of them.

No, they wanted to be in charge, and some seemed to get off on rough-handling someone half their size, as Myron had discovered. Assholes. That was why he stayed away from huge men and made do with people who couldn't physically overpower him. Not as much fun, but safety first. He'd gotten lucky that one time he'd been able to get away, but that didn't mean he'd escape next time.

It left him frustrated, as usual. Fighting against stereotypes seemed to be the story of his life, but god, he was so fucking sick and tired of it. "You're off the hook, okay? Your ass is safe," he snapped.

Abel blinked. "What if I don't want to be off the hook?"

What if he...? What the fuck was he saying? He wasn't making any sense. "What do you mean?"

Abel sat straight, his brown eyes steeling with resolve. "I want you to have a go at my ass."

Myron's heart skipped a beat. "You said it was the only spot on your body that didn't have ink other than your face."

"I did, and it's true."

"You said, and I quote, that hell would freeze over before you allowed anyone to even get close to your virgin ass."

"I know what I said."

"Last time I checked, hell was still hot, so what gives?"

Abel shrugged, but he didn't quite pull off indifference, not with his eyes as burning as they were. But why? "I changed my mind."

"You changed your mind. Like, that's it? That's the whole explanation?"

"It's a full sentence, isn't it?"

Myron shook his head. "That makes zero sense to me. Even if you did want someone to ink your ass, why on earth would you pick me? You don't even like me."

"You're crazy talented," Abel said softly.

Warmth lit up inside Myron. "Thank you, but that doesn't answer my question."

"You asked why I would choose you. Isn't the fact that you're talented enough reason?"

"With anyone else, yes, but not with you. Dude, I've somehow irritated you since the first time we met, and don't even try to deny it. Why would you want someone you hate to ink you?"

"Because you're that good? Besides, I don't hate you."

"You don't?" Myron was taken aback. "So I have imagined all those dirty looks?"

Abel snorted. "Like you've been nice to me. Every time

you so much as glance in my direction, you're scowling. If you got me glaring at you, it must've been a reaction to your utter lack of charm."

"I scowl at everybody. Not a people person. What else can I say?"

A frown marred Abel's forehead. "You're saying it wasn't directed at me?"

"I don't like people, for the most part, and big men even less. Bad experience and all that. And angry is kind of my default setting, so don't take it personally."

"Oh."

Had he really thought Myron was angry at him specifically? "You thought I had it out for you?"

After a long pause, Abel said, "Yes, I was convinced you did. You're so cocky and arrogant, and you always shoot daggers in my direction."

Myron rolled his eyes. "I have to project confidence. Do you have any idea how hard it is to be taken seriously when you look like me? Especially compared to someone like you, who much better fits the stereotype of a tattoo artist."

"But you're beautiful," Abel blurted out, then froze.

His words hung in the room, twirling around in Myron's head, then sinking deep into his heart. Abel thought he was beautiful? And he'd been convinced Myron had hated him? Had he been wrong about this whole situation? Just how straight was Abel?

Myron cocked his head, studying Abel with whole new eyes. "You said you wanted me to have a go at your ass. What exactly are we talking about here?"

3

Nothing in this conversation was going the way Abel had expected it to. But then again, this was Myron, the one man who always managed to throw him off-kilter, to make his tongue all tied and twisted and his stomach in knots. But how could he answer this question without giving it all away?

It had been two years since he'd met Myron at a tattoo convention. Two years since those baby blues had been trained on him for the first time, so cool and confident. Two years since he'd realized he wasn't straight because he sure as fuck had never felt about a woman the way he felt about Myron. Two years since he'd lost his heart and maybe a little of his sanity because he hadn't been able to get him out of his mind.

Myron had said he didn't hate him. Abel clung to that, which was ridiculous because there was a wide gap between not hating and wanting him the way he craved Myron, and yet it would have to do. He had to take the next step, or he would go crazy. He couldn't endure another two years of aching for him, of pining like a lovesick teenager.

"We're talking about my ass and you having a go at it...in any way you like."

He couldn't believe he'd said it, but the words were out now.

Myron's eyes widened in shock. "I thought you were straight."

"So did I until I met you."

They grew as wide as saucers. "You're shitting me."

Now that the truth was out, Abel felt lighter and surprisingly bold. "Nope. One look at you made me realize I was very much not straight."

They stared at each other, eyes burning, and Abel's gut churning. Then Myron got up, ambled over to the door, kicked it shut, and locked it from the inside. Abel sat frozen to his chair as Myron sauntered over, all limbs and angles, yet as graceful as a panther stalking his prey.

"You *like* me," he drawled.

"I'm crazy attracted to you," Abel corrected him. "Not sure about the liking part yet."

"I'm not a woman."

"Trust me, I've noticed."

"Have you ever been with a man?"

Abel shook his head. "Went to a gay bar, curious to see if my newfound bisexual awakening extended to men in general, but it seems to be limited to only you. So far."

Myron pushed Abel's chair back, and he helped him by using his feet, the legs scraping over the linoleum floor. What was Myron doing? Blue eyes held his as Myron lowered himself onto Abel's lap.

Oh, Jesus, his cock was taking an immediate interest, recognizing the object of his obsession of the last two years. How many times had he jacked off, dreaming of Myron?

Something told him reality was about to top every fantasy he'd ever had.

"So now that you have me, so to speak, what do you want to do to me?" Myron said, his voice low and husky.

Abel lifted his arm and dragged his index finger down Myron's cheek, past his sharp jawbone, down his neck, which was covered with a sleeve-tattoo of an abstract monster, dark and menacing and endlessly fascinating to watch as he moved. "Who did this? It's exquisite."

Myron grinned devilishly. "You have me on your lap, and you wanna talk shop? Maybe you're more straight than you thought."

He was flat out baiting him, but Abel was tired of fighting him, of battling the desire that had run through his veins for so long. And so he curled his hand around that fragile neck, pulled gently, and kissed him. Myron's lips were soft, so soft, unlike anything else about him, but Abel liked that. They melted to his, pliant for now, though that wouldn't last long, most likely.

He took his time kissing him, roaming his mouth with his tongue, nibbling on his lips, reveling in how sharp he tasted, minty mixed in with coffee. Myron's eyes had fluttered shut, and oh, how young he looked now, uncharacteristically vulnerable. "You're so pretty," Abel whispered against his lips.

Those blue eyes flew open, drilling into Abel's as if verifying he was speaking the truth. Then he growled, yanking Abel closer. "I don't do slow," he said almost defensively and kissed Abel.

Abel was no longer in charge, that much was clear, but he surrendered willingly as Myron grabbed his hair with both hands, almost painfully tugging on it as he kissed him with a raw passion that left him reeling. Myron gyrated his hips, his weight pressed down on Abel's cock.

He moaned way too loudly, but Myron swallowed most of the sound as he did it again, a wicked gleam in his eyes. "You're big."

"Yeah." What was the use of denying it? He had every intention of letting Myron find out, though preferably not in the break room of a tattoo shop.

"How big?"

"Seven inches, but I'm thick."

"Mmm, I like the sound of that."

He looked at Abel as if he was waiting for something, as if there was something Abel was supposed to say or do. He had no idea what, and so he kept quiet. He'd encountered Myron's temper too often to risk setting him off.

"You're not gonna say it?" Myron asked through gritted teeth.

"I don't know what you want me to say."

"When a gay man tells you he likes the sound of your fat cock, the logical next step would be to offer him an up close and personal encounter, usually worded along the lines of 'Wanna fuck?' or similar."

Oh. The thought hadn't even occurred to him. "I wasn't there yet."

"Don't tell me you need three dates first. I don't date. I fuck."

That defensive, almost hostile tone was intended to scare him off. Abel was certain of it, but he found it hot. What that meant for his mental stability, he'd rather not think about too long. "No, I don't need three dates, but five minutes ago, I thought you hated my guts, so I need a little more time to get with the program. That, and I do prefer a more comfortable location."

Myron studied him, then gave him a last, hard kiss and slid off his lap. "Give me your phone."

Abel didn't even consider protesting. He dug his phone out of his back pocket, unlocked it, and handed it over. Myron's thumbs flew over the keyboard, and then he dropped it back into Abel's hand. "I put in my address. Tonight, eight p.m. Don't be late."

4

He never invited men to his apartment anymore, not after a bad experience with a Grindr hookup that had resulted in Myron locking himself in his bathroom and calling 911. Some people just wouldn't take no for an answer, and that asshole had definitely been one of those. He'd had a good hundred pounds on Myron, and he'd barely gotten away from him before the guy could inflict some real damage. After that, he'd never let strange men into his apartment, and he'd seldom hooked up with bigger guys.

But somehow, he trusted Abel, despite his imposing size. The fact that he was a renowned tattoo artist with a solid reputation helped. Surely, if he'd been a sexually aggressive asshole, that rumor would've made the rounds. Besides, Reid trusted him, and that spoke volumes, since he rarely was wrong about people. The list of people Myron both liked and respected was a short one, but Reid was at the very top.

And good lord, Abel was so fucking perfect. The man had to be over six feet two, and he was built like a wall, all strong muscles under alluring roundness, with that sexy hair. He was brown with a ginger undertone, and it showed in the freckles on his face. Would he have those anywhere else? Or would they all have been covered by his tattoos?

Myron had a lot of ink, from his neck down to his arms and chest, as well as a few on his legs. But his back was still empty, a blank canvas for someone to use. Abel, however, had ink all over his body. Animals were the theme. He had an eagle on his shoulders, a bear on his chest, a massive lion draped around his right thigh, and snakes circling his calves. Myron wanted to lick each and every one of them. Not that he would, considering this would be a hookup. If the man showed, that was, but Myron had a gut feeling he would.

At eight on the dot, the front door buzzed, and a quick check through the peephole confirmed it was Abel. Myron let him in, taking a moment to admire that big body packed into a pair of tight jeans and a black T-shirt that spanned across his chest. Abel took off his shoes, an endearing gesture that made Myron way mushier inside than he liked.

"Hi," Abel said, stuffing his hands into his pockets.

He smelled fresh, woodsy, with a pine undertone, which had to be his body wash. Myron had planned to attempt a normal conversation with the guy before jumping him, seeing as how he was new at this and all, but fuck all that. Talking was overrated.

He leaped at him, and Abel scrambled to catch him just as Myron wrapped his legs around his waist and latched himself onto Abel's mouth. The man let out the most beautiful groan, all low and growly. Myron kissed him until he was out of breath. "Bedroom?"

He managed to make it sound like a question, even though his instinct was to leave no room for discussion.

Hello, he was fucking dying to get his greedy little hands on this delectable man. But even though he'd seemed okay with Myron taking the lead, he didn't want to push too hard.

"Yes."

Abel's answer was firm, sending a flare of heat through Myron's body. "Carry me?"

Abel grinned. "Gladly."

"First door on the right."

Abel walked, holding him tightly, those massive hands spread under Myron's ass. Mmm, that felt good. The man had such a strong grip, his fingers digging into Myron's flesh. How would it feel to control that?

He was the biggest slob on the planet, but he'd taken a few minutes to tidy his bedroom, even making the bed. And hoping for the best, he'd put the lube and some condoms on the little table next to his bed. Looked like he was about to get lucky.

He'd expected Abel to dump him on the bed, but the man lowered him slowly, then spread out on top of him, pinning him with his body. So damn hot, all that controlled strength pressing down on him. Abel let go for a moment and pushed himself up, then whipped his T-shirt over his head. Holy fuck, that chest... Myron could barely refrain from drooling. Instead, he ditched his shirt as well.

"Can I?" Abel pointed at the skinny jeans Myron was wearing.

"Fuck, yes. Undress me, big guy."

Abel's hands were surprisingly nimble and soft as they peeled Myron out of his jeans and took off his socks, leaving him in a pair of pink briefs that hugged his hard dick. A wet spot was already forming near his waistband, courtesy of his leaking cock.

Abel gazed at him as if he wanted to eat Myron, maybe

lick him all over, and hell yes, he was so down with that. "You're breathtaking," Abel said hoarsely, and Myron's belly did a little flop.

"Thank you. You can touch, you know."

"Give me a moment."

"Why?"

Abel rolled his eyes. "'Cause I'll blow my load in thirty seconds if I touch you right now. I've been dreaming about this for a long time, you know."

"You have?" The thought was hot. "What kind of dreams?"

"The very detailed kind that had me wake up panting and jacking off."

"Ohhhh, that sounds like you had some good fantasies going there."

"So far, the reality surpasses my wildest dreams."

Why did he keep saying mushy shit like that? Myron liked it, but it also made him uncomfortable, as if Abel was attaching far more meaning to this than the simple hookup it was supposed to be. Myron didn't do relationships. He'd had the worst example possible in the two people who had the dubious honor of bringing him into the world, and he had zero desire to end up as unhappy as them. Nope, he'd be single and free without all that relationship shit and drama dragging him down.

Abel kneeled on the carpet, gently spreading Myron's legs. Myron leaned backward on his elbows so he could watch Abel as he kissed his right foot, then made a slow, thorough trail up the inside of his leg. He traced his tattoos with his tongue, licking and tasting him everywhere. God, the man was nothing if not thorough.

Finally, he reached the apex of his thigh, the edge of his briefs, and he nuzzled it, breathing in deeply as his beard tickled Myron's skin. "I can smell you," Abel whispered. "Your arousal. I can smell it."

"Do you like it?"

"I love it."

He pressed soft kisses on the inside of his thigh, then crossed over to his other leg. Myron groaned as he started another path there, beginning at his foot again. "Could we maybe skip ahead?"

Abel looked up, his eyes dark with lust. "No. I don't know if you'll ever allow me the opportunity again, so I want to take my time with this."

That shut Myron right up. Abel wanted to do this again? How could he know this when they'd only just started? He needed to think about this, but that was hard when Abel set his body on fire with every kiss of his firm, hot lips, every touch of his callused hands, every scratch of that gorgeous beard, every fiery look from eyes that looked like black pools. Abel was seducing him, one step at a time, and Myron didn't know how to stop it.

But the bigger question was, why would he even want to when it felt so goddamn good?

5

———

Impatience simmered in Myron's body, in his eyes, but Abel ignored it. He hadn't been lying. He'd ached to explore every inch of this beautiful man, and by god, he would, knowing all too well that he might never get the chance again. He worked his way up his leg, then jumped to his belly, dragging him lower on the bed. Myron made a sound of protest, raising his hips in a gesture that was nowhere near subtle, but Abel pretended he didn't see it.

He tongued Myron's belly button, then licked his way up to that smooth, hairless chest, tracing tattoo lines with his tongue, his fingers, sometimes his teeth. Myron's nipples were tight buds, dark pink, and how sweet they tasted. Almost as sweet as the sounds Myron made when Abel sucked on them, scratched them with his teeth, then soothed them again.

More hip movements and a needy sigh, but Abel still wasn't done. The top of Myron's shoulders was bare, a strip of ivory white skin showing between his neck sleeve and the intricate pattern tattooed on his chest. Gorgeous.

By the time he was satisfied he'd seen every bit of skin

except what was hiding under those tented briefs, Myron was moaning and grunting, moving restlessly. Abel smiled as he returned to his mouth for a thorough, lazy kiss.

"You done exploring now?" Myron asked. They lay stretched out on the bed, on their sides, facing each other. "Can we move on to the next step?"

Abel's smile widened. "Yeah."

Myron hesitated. "What do you want?"

Abel had an idea of why Myron would ask, a gut instinct. He might not have experience with gay sex, but he had plenty of gay friends and had learned a lot over the years. One thing his best friend, David, had stressed was that you couldn't tell sexual preferences just from someone's body type. David was slender, but he very much preferred topping over bottoming...and Abel had a feeling Myron was the same way. He liked to be in charge, even though he was letting Abel lead.

"Why don't you take charge?" he suggested as he tucked a wild lock of hair behind his ear. "You're the one with experience here."

"Right." Myron bit his lip. "But I still need to know what you want. I mean, I assume you have a firm grasp of the positions involved?"

"I do, but I'm fine either way."

Myron gaped at him. "You are? You'd be willing to bottom?"

"Sure. I'm told it feels very good when done right, and you seem like someone who'd make sure I get pleasure from it, so..."

"What the hell are you basing that on? You don't even know me."

"I've watched you put ink on someone. You're a perfectionist. Your designs and your technique are flawless. I can't imagine you being any different when it comes to sex."

Myron eyed him. "You've given this a lot of thought."

"Well, when you invited me over, I was kinda hoping it would lead to this, so yeah, I did think things through. I'm not what people would call an impulsive person."

"I didn't think you were. For what it's worth, I've been told I'm a generous lover, so you were on the right track."

"Then my virgin ass is yours in every way. All you need to do is decide if you want to fuck it first...or ink it."

Myron threw his head back and laughed. "Easy choice, big guy. Fuck it thoroughly and then ink it. And if I remember correctly, I get to pick the design too."

Abel nodded. "That was the bet. My bare ass and a design of your choice."

Myron's laugh faded into something far more serious. "I can't believe you'd let me top you."

"Why not?"

"Erm, because of our body types and the expected role patterns that come with it?"

Abel shrugged. "I've never cared what people think, and this is no different. You're a bossy little shit, and I like that. I'm happy to put you in charge."

"Really?"

"Sure, why the hell not? I've had no issues in the past with strong women who wanted to have their way with me."

Myron's face lit up in a way he'd never seen before, and it took his breath away. He beamed, almost like he was a magical creature, an elf or a fae of some kind with his pale skin and all those amazing tattoos. "I promise I'll make it good for you."

A mask fell over his face again, closing him off, as if he realized he'd shown too much. But Abel had seen it now, the sweetness hidden underneath. He'd do whatever it took to unearth that again.

Myron reached for him, and Abel let him, allowing himself to be pushed onto his back. Myron rolled on top of him. Their mouths found each other again for a sloppy, uncoordinated kiss. Myron fumbled with Abel's belt and undid it, then flicked the button of his jeans open and pushed down the zipper. He slid his hand lower, cupping Abel's rock-hard cock, and he couldn't hold back the moan that rose inside him.

"Mmm, let's get you undressed, big guy."

Myron slithered down on the bed and pulled Abel's jeans off as he watched him through heavy-lidded eyes. So beautiful. So fierce and feral, like a wild horse you had to work hard to gain its trust. Would Abel ever be able to tame him? He'd have to go slow and oh-so careful.

His underwear came off at the same time as his jeans, and Myron made quick work of the last few items of clothing. He pushed Abel's legs wide and tapped them until Abel got the message and pulled them up, spreading them wide. A quick grab from the nightstand and Myron's slick fingers found his crack, sliding back and forth to prepare him for what was coming next.

Abel tensed. Myron must have felt it because while his right hand was still massaging his hole, he caressed his balls with his left, then cradled them one by one. Distracted, Abel relaxed again, and before he knew it, a warm finger pressed against his hole.

This, too, he'd heard enough times to know what to do, and he let him in, gasping as Myron sunk inside him. Oh, that was a new feeling... Not unpleasant, though it stung a little.

"Goddamn, your ass is clenching my finger," Myron

whispered, sounding almost in awe. "You're gonna feel so good around my cock."

Abel's insides grew all warm. Who knew it would be arousing to hear someone praise him like that? He couldn't spend too much time thinking about it because Myron's hands got busy, and the man was clearly ambidextrous, his left hand as skilled in exploring Abel's balls, then his cock, as his right was in working him open.

He let it happen, allowed the strange sensations to wash over him. His ass was burning, but in a good way, sending sparks throughout his body. He'd never known he had so many nerve endings there and that they were connected to everything else. He was breathless and panting, his cock leaking like crazy.

Myron played with his precum, spreading it around with his thumb, creating all kinds of slick, sexy noises as he teased his slit, his crown. Almost as sexy as the sounds he made, humming in approval, sighing, moaning. He was vocal, and Abel loved it.

When Myron had managed to get three fingers in without Abel tensing up, he knew it was time. And indeed, Myron withdrew his fingers and sat back, kneeling on the bed between Abel's legs. "You ready?"

6

Myron held his breath. Abel was so perfect, the way he lay there on the bed, that big, strong, furry body as soft as putty in Myron's hands. He wanted him so fiercely it scared him. He loved sex, loved hooking up, but when was the last time he'd been so into it, so restless and impatient to be inside someone?

Abel hadn't given any indication he had changed his mind, but it was still his first time with a man, and bottoming at that. Myron had to allow for the possibility that Abel would back out, though he didn't think so.

Abel met Myron's gaze, those brown eyes steady and confident. "Have at it."

Have at it. How could three simple words be so incredibly arousing? They fired him up, sinking deep inside him, into his very soul. They had weight, somehow. Significance. As if Abel was saying much more than he was letting on.

Myron shook his head to chase those strange and disturbing thoughts away. This was a hookup. Nothing else, nothing more. Just sex. Really good sex, hopefully. It certainly had the potential to be spectacular, what with how tight and hot Abel's ass was.

He shoved a pillow under Abel's ass to get a better angle, rolled a condom over his cock, and positioned himself. "Bear down on me," he said and pushed.

Abel's hole resisted, but then the man sighed and let him in. Myron slipped past that first ring of muscle, the tip of his cock engulfed in the hottest, tightest place it had ever been in. He halted, sweat breaking out all over his body as he fought the need to go hard and deep. "You good?" he checked.

"Yeah."

The unspoken plea to go slow was crystal clear, and Myron had every intention of doing that. He didn't often encounter virgins anymore, or at least anal virgins, but he'd had a few, and he'd always taken care to proceed with caution, doing whatever he could to make it a good experience for them.

He did the same now, thrusting shallowly as he sank in inch by inch. His cock was longer than average—though not as big as Abel's—but he was thin, making it a little easier to take. And oh, it felt good, that tight heat hugging his cock. He didn't even have the urge to thrust. All he wanted was to stay inside him, have his cock buried inside Abel's strong body.

When he bottomed out, Abel let out a shivery sigh. "That went easier than I had expected."

"Feel good?"

"A little strange and there's some stinging, but you brushed past a spot that holds the key to make me explode in bliss, so let's do this."

Myron snickered at the dry way Abel had worded that. "I've got you, big guy."

He went slow and careful, making long, precise strokes, watching Abel intently for his reaction. He was frowning as if he was concentrating on his body, trying to determine what he was feeling, but then Myron altered the angle, and Abel's expression changed. He closed his eyes, his mouth dropped open, and the most beautiful sound rumbled up from his chest.

Myron put a bit more force behind his thrusts, snapping his hips as he drove into Abel with precision. "Oh, fuck," Abel moaned and snaked his right hand between them, circling his cock.

Myron sped up, making sure to keep that same angle, since he seemed to have hit the proverbial jackpot. Bliss crawled up from his balls, up his spine, then down his arms all the way to his fingertips. Sometimes it would crash over him, but this time, it built slowly, pushing his body higher and higher.

"Harder," Abel grunted, and it was music to Myron's ears.

He surged into him, putting his weight behind it, his balls slapping against Abel's hot skin.

"Ohgodohfuckohmotherofgod..."

Myron smiled, then did it again.

Abel was jacking himself off, his cheeks red, drops of sweat pearling on his forehead, and his breaths coming out in puffs. His hair was matted against his head, his eyes glassy and unfocused, as if he was seeing something far beyond what was right in front of him.

Myron was panting too, his muscles growing tired as his heart pounded to a rapid beat, his blood singing with need. Harder. Faster. Deeper. He obeyed its call, and when Abel moaned low and deep, seemingly lost to the world, Myron let go. He pumped into him, his hips driving with force, his ass contracting.

His balls clenched tight against his body, humming and buzzing, ready to unload. The base of his cock started to tingle, a telltale sign he was oh-so close, but one look at Abel confirmed he was too. He'd thrown his head back now, his hand furiously fisting his crown.

Myron couldn't tear his eyes away from the man who was lost in pleasure, surrendering fully. Abel's body went tense, jerking underneath him, and Myron halted.

"Unnnngh..." Abel groaned as a thick rope of cum flew from his cock all over his hand and dripped onto his stomach. "Oh god..."

Myron kept watching, unable to look away as Abel came and came until he finally went slack. His eyes drifted open, still unfocused. Then he found Myron. A lazy, sweet smile spread over his swollen lips. "That was fucking amazing."

"I could tell."

Myron pulled out, knowing from experience he'd better do that now while Abel was still blissed out. He kneeled between his legs, rolled off the condom, took his cock in his right hand, and jacked himself off. His orgasm washed over him like a sweet relief, his whole body shuddering and shivering as his cock unloaded, spurting all over Abel's stomach, mixing in with the man's own cum. Marking him, and why that felt so insanely good, Myron didn't want to think about too much.

He wanted to crash, too tired to even lift a finger, but he couldn't. Not after this. And so he crawled from the bed. "Hang on," he told Abel.

He threw the condom into the trash bin, then got a washcloth from the bathroom. He cleaned Abel's stomach first while the man watched him with intense eyes. Then he refreshed the cloth and cleaned himself, then Abel's ass. When he was done, he threw the washcloth onto the bathroom floor.

Abel was stretched out on the bed, all six-foot-something of him, and Myron's belly went weak. He was so damn hot. He hesitated, then told himself to stop being ridiculous and lay down next to him. As if they'd done it a million times before, Abel wrapped his arm around Myron and pulled him close. Myron fought it for a few seconds, then gave in and crawled closer until he lay with his head on Abel's shoulder.

"So," Abel said, and his low voice rumbled through his chest. "When can we do this again?"

7

He should've kept his mouth shut. Abel stared at his phone, which had been busy enough with calls and messages, but none of them from the one person he'd wanted to hear from. A week had passed since he and Myron had hooked up and not even a peep. As much as Abel hated to admit that what he'd felt had apparently been one-sided, he had no choice, since Myron's quick method of making Abel leave had made it crystal clear it had been just sex for him.

If he hadn't told him he was down for a repeat, would Myron have bolted from the room? Would he have gotten dressed that quickly and ushered Abel out the door with an efficiency that betrayed a lot of experience? For Abel, their encounter had been earth-shattering. Life-changing. He'd kissed the stars and had embraced the whole universe, but more than that, he'd realized he'd fallen hard and fast for Myron.

He was thirty-six, and for years, he'd wondered if he'd ever meet his someone special. He'd dated plenty of women, but none of them had ever made him feel more than attraction, sometimes mixed in with affection. But gentle affection, the kind you had for a friend, a nice neighbor. Not the kind of intense, bordering-on-obsessive way he felt about Myron. Just his luck that he'd lost his heart to the one guy who didn't want it.

So what did he do now? He could text him, but his gut said Myron would either ignore it or answer it in the most standoffish way, aimed at keeping Abel at a distance. No, that wouldn't get him anywhere. So what would?

An idea popped into his head, and he knew it would be his best shot. It had worked before, hadn't it? He didn't overthink it and got dressed, then left, heading for Rainbow Ink. Today was his day off, so he might as well make good use of his time.

When he walked in, he immediately sought Myron out in the back. An elastic band held his hair off his forehead, and he was inking someone, concentrating on whatever he was creating on the woman's upper arm.

"You're back." Mari turned off her needle, looking at him quizzically. "I assume you're here for Myron again?"

"Yeah, but I'll wait until he's done."

She pursed her lips. "If you're the reason he's been in such a pissy mood all week, it might not be the best idea to confront him here."

"He was in a bad mood?"

Abel didn't know why, but a happy flutter danced in his stomach. Maybe Myron hadn't been unaffected either? Unless his mood was completely unrelated, but somehow, he doubted that.

Mari rolled her eyes. "The worst. He's never Mr. Sunshine, but this week has been horrific, what between the thunderclouds hanging over his head and the news about Reid's sister."

Abel frowned. "Reid's sister? The one who was getting married?"

"Yup, that one. She called off the wedding the day before. Reid was in a state, let me tell you. He was the one who had to tell her groom."

"Damn." Abel scratched his beard. "Poor guy. That's like the ultimate humiliation. Well, except being actually being left at the altar, but this was close enough."

"I know. And Reid is caught between a rock and a hard place because he's quite fond of him, it seems, but he also wants to be loyal to his sister. Anyway, face Myron at your own peril."

Abel nodded in understanding, then sat down on a comfortable sofa chair, pulled out his Kindle, and settled in to read.

It took an hour for Myron to finish up with his client. He walked to the front with her, sharing instructions on how to take care of her new ink. "And make sure to keep it out of the sun for the first few weeks. Sunlight is your worst enemy."

His eyes fell on Abel, and he halted for a moment, then caught himself and held the door open for her.

"Thank you so much. It looks amazing," the woman said.

"My pleasure. You have my card, so contact me if you have any issues."

"I will."

With a last wave, she walked out, and as soon as she was gone, Myron spun around, a scowl on his face. "What are you doing here?"

"I'm here for my appointment for you to ink my ass," Abel said calmly.

Myron blinked. "I'm... That's... I have appointments all day."

"That's okay. I'll wait." Abel showed his Kindle. "I came prepared. I even brought snacks."

Myron stared at him for a few seconds longer, as if he expected Abel to cower under his menacing look. It made him laugh, though he manfully held it in. As if he would ever be afraid of someone who looked like a fucking elf.

"If you wanna waste an entire day here, be my guest," Myron mumbled and stalked off.

With a grin, Abel settled in his chair again. Myron cleaned his booth with disinfectant, then got everything ready for his next client. He worked methodically as he prepared his workstation, covering his tray with plastic film, setting out a razor, paper towels, the needle packs, the ink caps with various colors—lots of greens and browns for this particular client—the ointment. Everything was meticulously laid out and cleaned. Not that Abel had had any doubts about the hygienic standards of Rainbow Ink, but it was good to see it confirmed.

Myron's client was a guy in a suit, and they'd clearly met before. Myron was even smiling at him. Abel watched with fascination as the man peeled off his corporate dress shirt, revealing an amazing work in progress on his chest. A tree, intricate and fascinating, with branches and leaves and little twigs. Abel couldn't stop staring at it, even though it was hard to see from where he sat.

So why not come a little closer and watch Myron at work? He walked over to his booth, and the guy in the suit turned around. "Hi," Abel said, pasting a friendly smile on his face. "I'm here to observe Myron. Would you mind if I sit in on this session to watch?"

The guy shrugged. "Not at all."

Abel ignored the annoyance that rolled off Myron in waves and grabbed a stool. He made sure he sat far enough away to not be in the way while still being close enough to see everything. Myron had apparently decided to pretend Abel wasn't there, but that didn't deter Abel.

Myron adjusted the tattoo table so the man's chest was at the right height, and got to work. Ah, he was adding color to the linework he'd done in an earlier session, or more than one, considering the size of the tattoo. With precise fingers, he colored in the trunk, then the branches, before moving on to all kinds of green for the leaves. The whole design was stunning, and Abel was entranced.

Myron chatted with the client, first somewhat stilted, but then more freely as they discovered a similar taste in music and bands and shared stories of festivals and concerts they had attended. Meanwhile, he worked fast and precise, the buzzing of his needle as familiar to Abel as his own body.

What would it feel like to have Myron tattoo him? What had been an impulsive, drunken bet, fueled by his two-year pent-up frustration of a one-sided attraction, was now becoming a real desire. He was extremely picky about who got to ink him, only working with people he trusted as much as he trusted himself.

But watching Myron work, one thing became crystal clear. He did trust him, and he wanted him to have a go at his ass. With a needle, but hopefully also for a repeat performance with his cock. A man could dream, right?

8

Myron would never admit it out loud, but he loved that Abel was watching him. He never said a word, but his expressive face showed his admiration for what Myron was doing, and that quiet approval sank deep inside him. It meant something to him, coming from someone he respected so much. God, Abel DiRossi was a fucking legend in the tattoo world, and he had a waiting list that was at least a year long.

But more than that, the opinion of the man himself mattered far more than Myron had expected. They were rivals. Competitors. And yes, they had hooked up once, and yes, it had been amazing sex, but so what? He'd had great sex before, right?

Though he'd never had a man look at him the way Abel had, as if he was something precious and special, something valuable that needed to be treasured. And he'd certainly never had a man surrender to him like Abel had, that strong body so pliant and willing. What a rush it had been to top him and bring him so much pleasure.

No, as much as he wanted to pretend Abel was just

another hookup, he was anything but. If he had been, Myron wouldn't have spent all week thinking about him, wondering how he could reach out to him without making it seem like he wanted more, then getting frustrated with himself because he couldn't find a way.

He finished tattooing Gio, then quickly got everything ready for his next client, which was a short job—just a quote she wanted on her forearm. He didn't usually do those, but he'd done all her tattoos, so he couldn't say no.

Once she was done, he closed the front door behind her and locked it, then walked back to his booth. Mari and Hao had left already, and so it was only him and Abel. Abel was quiet as Myron tidied and cleaned, but his eyes were constantly on him, observing his every move.

"Come here," Abel said when Myron had finished and thrown his gloves into the trash.

Myron hesitated but then went over. Abel was gentle as he pulled him between his broad legs. "You're in charge," he said softly.

Myron frowned. "What do you mean?"

"I want to see you again, but I won't push. The ball is in your court, and it will stay there. You're in charge here."

Myron's head dazzled with the implications of that statement. "Why would you do that?"

Abel caressed his cheeks with his index fingers, his eyes so soft and sweet. "When I was a child, my parents took me on a vacation to some dude ranch in Montana where we spent the whole week learning about horses. One of the guys was taming a horse, and day after day, he'd stand for hours in the paddock with him, working on earning his trust. He never pressured him, never forced him, but always allowed the horse to come to him. He said he'd been at it for three weeks already, and every day, he was getting a little closer. On the last day we were there, the horse finally came to him and ate an apple from his hand."

Where was he going with this? Myron wanted to ask, but the patient look in Abel's eyes had him hold back a snappy remark.

"You remind me of that horse. Just as skittish and stubborn. Just as determined to stay away from me and remain wild and free."

Myron's throat tightened. Why was he so moved by this? It was just a stupid story, a weird analogy that was somehow eerily accurate and sweet. He swallowed. "So what does that mean?"

Another caress and then Abel pulled him in for a brief kiss. "It means that I'll be standing here with an apple or a sugar cube or whatever you want, patiently waiting until you trust me enough to come to me. I've waited two years for you to notice me, to really see me, and I can wait two more if I have to."

"T-two years?" What was Abel saying?

"Mmm. I fell for you the moment I saw you, and trust me, I've tried to forget about you, but it was useless."

"I'm not a nice person. Like, I'm snappy and often irritated, and my temper has a short fuse."

Abel grinned. "Do you think you're telling me something new? Two years of you glaring at me haven't managed to dissuade me so far, so that doesn't help either. You're a prickly cactus, but apparently I have a thing for prickly cacti, so there you have it."

Irrational frustration rose in him. "I told you all I wanted was sex. A hookup. I don't do relationships, and I certainly don't do love or some shit."

"I heard you. But *I* do, and it's all I have to offer. Oh, don't get me wrong. I'll take the sex for now, since it was spectacular, but I'll never cease asking for more. Not until you tell me to stop."

A mix of anger and bafflement bubbled inside him. How dare Abel offer him that? How could this man not only want him but *like* him too? He couldn't grasp it, no matter how he tried. "I...I don't know what to say."

"You don't need to say anything."

"I wanna fuck you again."

Abel's eyes were too kind. "I was hoping you would. Your place or mine?"

"Mine." That way, he could kick him out if it got too much.

"What about my tattoo?"

Myron shook his head. "I can't do it now. Not when I'm like this. Besides, you haven't decided on the design yet."

"I told you that's up to you. You'll pick something amazing. I watched you work again today, and I'm so in awe of your talent. You'll create a masterpiece on my hairy ass."

Myron chuckled. "I'd better take the time to shave it really well."

"I have all the time in the world for you when you're ready."

9

The second time they'd had sex had been as spectacular as the first round, but on this occasion, Abel had been smart enough not to mention he wanted more. He'd left as soon as Myron had started getting restless, telling him once again that if he wanted to hook up again, he'd have to reach out.

Oh, it cost him to wait, and after five days, he wondered if he'd made a mistake. Had he misjudged their sexual chemistry? Myron had to have a wide choice of men available to him, so was it arrogance to assume he'd pick Abel?

Then he got the text.

I'm free tonight. Wouldn't mind fucking you again if you're in the mood.

Aw, he was such a romantic.

I can squeeze you in. What time?

8?

Works for me. See you then.

K.

He'd been summoned, and despite the aloofness in Myron's text, Abel was counting down the hours. He showered, shaved, did some extra cleaning for Myron's benefit, and got dressed. He ran Myron's buzzer at eight sharp.

"You're annoyingly punctual," Myron said as he let him in.

"Annoyingly? I thought being punctual was a good habit."

"It is, but..." Myron waved his hand. "Never mind."

They stood in the hallway, Myron trying to cram his hands into the pockets of his skinny jeans and failing. "Do you want to...?" He gestured to the bedroom.

Inspiration struck Abel. "Actually, would you mind if I had a drink first? I'm thirsty. Had to rush to get here on time."

"Oh. Yeah, sure. What do you want?"

"Do you have beer?"

"I think I have some kind of weird brew from the last time Reid was here."

Abel had counted on Myron not being able to deny him that simple request. He'd have to be a massive asshole to refuse, and he wasn't. The more time he spent with Myron, the more Abel was convinced that his gruff exterior was just that: an exterior, a mask. He wasn't nearly as much of an asshole as he pretended to be.

"Are you and Reid...?" he asked when Myron came back with a bottle of beer and a glass of wine for himself.

"Fucking? Oh, hell no." Myron snorted. "I may not technically be his employee, but he certainly sees me that way, and he'd never do that. Not that I even want to sleep with him. I mean, he's hot, don't get me wrong, but he's my mentor. He's like an older brother, if I had any."

Abel sipped his beer. "You're an only child?"

"Yeah, thank fuck. My parents were..." Myron sighed, his

face tightening. "Let's just say they should never have had kids."

The last thing Abel wanted was for him to shut down, so he segued back to their earlier topic. "How did you end up at Rainbow Ink anyway?"

"I was taking some art classes, and Reid was a guest teacher for one of them, teaching charcoal drawing and how that transferred to tattoos. I was fascinated and asked him if I could stop by sometime and watch. I did, and I was hooked from the first tattoo I observed him do. He let me hang around the shop for a year, doing grunt work, before he agreed to teach me."

"You got lucky with a mentor like him. He's very good at what he does, but he's also a decent guy, and that's not always the case in our circles."

Myron rolled his eyes. "I know. I did a few internships in other shops to learn different techniques, and one guy refused to hear the word no. I had to quit before I finished the two weeks I was supposed to be there because he wouldn't fucking leave me alone."

"God, I'm so sorry." Should he ask for the guy's name? No, he'd better not. The tattoo world was a small one, and he couldn't guarantee he'd keep his head cool if he ran into the bastard.

Myron shrugged. "It happens. Not the first time. Won't be the last, probably."

It might not have been the topic Abel had wanted to discuss, but at least they were talking, and that was a step, right? All he wanted was for them to get to know each other better, for Myron to see him as more than just a hot body to fuck. But he'd learned from last time, and he wouldn't push his luck.

He finished his beer and met Myron's gaze. "Ready when you are."

Surely, there had to be a more elegant segue, some suave way to transition from this into sex, but he had no idea how, and with Myron so skittish already, the direct approach seemed the least risky.

"Oh." Myron eyed his wine glass, then drained it. "Okay."

He was nervous too. How had Abel missed it before? It was so obvious now. Myron masked it with his usual I-don't-give-two-fucks attitude, but underneath, he was as insecure as Abel. What a fascinating thought. Maybe Abel could help him by distracting him?

He rose from his seat and whipped his shirt over his head. Yup, he had Myron's attention, his eyes dropping to Abel's chest. Abel caressed his own pecs, even though he felt self-conscious and awkward, slid his hand down his chest, past his belly button, and dipped under the waistband of his jeans.

"Grab yourself," Myron said, his voice husky as he leaned back in his seat.

Abel did as he'd been told, putting his hand on his hardening cock and giving it a good squeeze.

"Mmm," Myron purred. "You're so big."

Abel stroked himself again, cursing the lack of space in his jeans.

"Take off your jeans."

Abel obeyed, all too happy to free himself from the confines of the rough fabric. The way he undressed might not be too sexy, but Myron didn't seem to care. His eyes were glued to Abel, who kicked off his jeans, took off his socks, and stood in his underwear. The tip of his cock peeked from the elastic waistband of his tight, white boxer briefs.

It had been a good many years since he was an athlete, playing hockey all through college, and he'd gained weight since then, but after seeing how Myron had looked at him the first time, he wasn't insecure about his physique. He was a bear in every way but the gray hair, which would undoubtedly arrive in a few years, and he was fine with it. His body was strong and healthy, and that was all that mattered.

"Take it out."

His whole body sizzled as he did what Myron told him, slipping his cock free and curling his hand around himself.

"Slowly fist yourself."

His breath hitched, his heart beating faster. His cock jumped in his hand, filling even more. Abel wasn't sure what was more arousing: fisting himself or the fiery, hungry look in Myron's eyes.

"Mmm, I wanna fucking eat you."

"That can be arranged." Hell, he'd kneel and offer himself any way Myron wanted him. Embarrassing, maybe, but he didn't care. He'd take him however he could have him.

"Take off your underwear."

Abel turned his back toward him and bent over as he dragged his boxers down, offering Myron a prime view of his ass. Myron moaned, low and deep. Somebody appreciated the view. Abel swiveled around, his cock standing at full mast now.

It felt strange, being naked while Myron was still dressed, though his erection tented his sweatpants, suggesting he'd gone commando. At the same time, it was arousing. Dirty, somehow. Maybe even a little demeaning and humiliating, especially considering who was in charge here, and yet Abel liked it. He liked doing what Myron told him, and so he stood and awaited further orders.

"Come here," Myron said, and Abel hurried over, his cock slapping against his stomach. Myron pointed where he wanted him—between his legs. Abel's cock was millimeters from his lips. Was he...?

Myron opened his mouth and, without preamble, sucked him in.

10

He hadn't planned to suck Abel off, but holy fuck, the guy looked downright edible, and Myron hadn't been able to contain himself. He loved sucking cock, but he rarely did it anymore, since it had become too personal for him, too intimate. Hand jobs were fine, and he'd fuck the shit out of the mouth or ass of anyone who asked, but he wouldn't reciprocate anymore.

Abel's cock tasted clean and fresh, evidence that the man had taken the time for some personal hygiene before coming over. When the first drop of precum hit Myron's tongue, he moaned. Fuck, he tasted so good.

The man hadn't been kidding when he'd said he had girth. Myron could barely fit him into his mouth, and taking him in deeper would be impossible, though he'd certainly love to try. He sucked on the tip, swirling his tongue, teasing Abel's slit, all while jacking him off with his hand.

Abel laced his hand through Myron's hair, pulling tight enough that a sharp pain shot through him, but it only fueled his need for more. What a rush to have this big body trembling under his hands, to have Abel fighting for control.

Myron had had every intention of burying himself inside Abel's tight ass again, but tasting his cock, he craved something else.

Cock.

He hadn't bottomed in a long time. Not because he hated it. He didn't. In fact, when done right, he loved bottoming almost as much as he loved topping. The problem was that usually the top was in charge, and he couldn't give up that control, not even when he bottomed. He hadn't met many men who would allow it, but Abel would. Abel would let Myron fuck himself on his fat cock until he sprayed his load all over him, and now that the thought had settled in his mind, Myron wanted it more than anything.

He wanted to use that perfect body to pleasure himself. To not have to worry about being too vulnerable or showing too much of himself. With Abel, the rules were clear, and he trusted him. He couldn't explain how or why, but he trusted him.

He pulled back, his jaw aching. "Bedroom."

Abel walked in front of him, and he slapped his butt playfully. Hmm, that left a bit of a red mark. Why was that so hot? He swatted his other ass cheek as well.

"Are we adding spanking to our repertoire?" Abel asked, humor lacing his voice.

"I don't know. I kinda like the sight of my handprint on your ass."

"Imagine what it would be like to see your tattoo there. Just saying. The offer still stands."

Heat flared up in Myron's belly. Abel was right. He would like to see his handiwork on his ass, but what would he put there? The design had to be right, the perfect choice for Abel, and Myron didn't have a clue of what that looked like.

"Where and how do you want me?" Abel stood right next to the bed.

Myron faced him, the top of his head grazing Abel's jaw. His thin hands looked so small compared to Abel's big ones, and Myron's whole body seemed half his size. And yet this man was so eager to follow Myron's instructions. Why did that mean so much to him?

"On the bed on your back," he told him. Abel climbed onto the bed and spread his legs wide in an open invitation to get fucked again, but Myron had other plans.

He couldn't do it with Abel watching him, though. That was too intimate, too close. He needed some distance from him. He pulled the one and only tie he owned from his closet and held it out to Abel. "Can I blindfold you?"

Abel swallowed, his brown eyes seeking reassurance in Myron's. "Yes."

"Okay."

He fastened the tie around Abel's eyes, testing to make sure he couldn't peek from underneath it. Only then did he undress. Shit, now he found himself in a predicament. How did he prep himself without Abel hearing the sounds and figuring things out? Myron didn't want him to know what was about to happen yet.

"I need a few minutes in the bathroom, but I promise I'll be back soon...and if you need anything, just call out."

"O-okay. Do you want me to do anything?"

How sweet was that? "Keep yourself rock hard, but don't make yourself come."

"I can do that."

Myron rushed into the bathroom, where he prepped himself with ruthless efficiency. There was nothing sexy about the way he worked himself open, but god knew he'd pay for sloppy prep if he took a cock that size. "You okay?" he called out to Abel.

"Yeah. Just...lonely?"

"Two more minutes."

He made it in under two, and when he walked back into the room, Abel was lazily fisting his cock, a long thread of precum dangling between his cock and his hand. If only Myron were a painter... He'd paint him like this and jack off to that image forever.

Instead, he grabbed a condom and more lube, then climbed onto the bed. Abel tensed when Myron swatted his hand away. He confidently rolled a condom over his gorgeous dick, and Abel gasped.

"Myron..."

"This okay?" He still had to ask, had to know Abel wanted this, even though he'd indicated before he was fine with either way.

"God, yes."

"Mmm... Gonna feast on your fat cock, big guy. Hold it up for me."

Abel held himself at the base, and Myron climbed on him, legs on either side of his thighs and ass wide open. He spread his ass cheeks as he sank down until the tip of Abel's cock hit his hole. He bore down, grunting as he worked himself downward, his ass on fire with every inch he took. Fuck, it was too much, too thick, and yet somehow perfect at the same time.

It took him a few minutes to get there. Fuck, it had been so long since he'd experienced that burn, that sting that radiated through his entire body, only to settle right back in his balls and at the base of his cock. Pleasure simmered there, interlaced with intense heat, and he broke out in a sweat.

"Fuck, Myron..." Abel groaned. "That feels... It's so fucking tight. So hot."

Right. It was his first time anal as a top. Myron had almost forgotten that, what with how accepting Abel seemed to be about the whole thing. He rubbed his hands over Abel's furry chest. "Yeah. You feeling good?"

Abel all but purred, a low sound that drifted up from his chest. "Fuck, yes. I'm so close already."

Myron smiled as he lifted his hips and screwed himself down. "You'd better keep that shit in check, big guy, because I need to have my way with you first."

"I promise," Abel said, his face and tone much more seriously than Myron had expected. "I won't ever let you down."

If only he could trust him in everything that easily.

11

Abel liked to think he was good at sex and always had been once he'd gotten through the first awkward stage in high school. He'd learned the female anatomy, had always made sure his partners got off too, had happily done oral, and over the years, he'd received many a compliment about his skills in bed.

But he sure as fuck had never felt like this. So...needy and wanton, so feverishly hot and restless, as if every cell in his body was connected to his dick. He wanted to fuck Myron, pound into him, claim him as his own. None of that made sense, but he trembled with the fierce need coursing through his veins.

"Please," he begged. "I wanna see you. I wanna see your pleasure."

Seconds later, warm fingers removed the tie, and he blinked against the light of the lamp on the nightstand. Myron leaned back, confidently sitting atop him, Abel's cock buried to the hilt inside him, and that thought alone was almost enough to make him come.

Myron raised his hips again and sank down, first going

slow and precise, but then as he seemed to have found the right position, harder and faster. Their bodies slapped together, the wet sound heavy in the room, mixing in with Myron's labored breaths.

Abel fisted the sheets, needing to hold on to something to prevent himself from flipping Myron over and taking charge. He couldn't, and he wouldn't, but oh, the urge was strong. But Myron needed to be in charge, that much had become clear, and so Abel fought and surrendered.

"Fuck, your cock is perfect," Myron panted. "So goddamn thick it splits my ass wide open. I don't think I've ever had someone this thick, and it feels fucking amazing."

"Thank you?" What else could he say? It wasn't like he'd picked out his body, though he had to admit he was damn proud of his dick and always had been. Definitely one of his best features.

Myron grinned. "You're so polite, even when you're balls deep inside me. It cracks me up."

He sped up again, and his expression changed into one of utter pleasure, his eyes darkening as he threw his head back. He wrapped his hand around his cock and jacked himself off, fast and furious.

Abel fought against his own body, trying to think of anything else but the sight in front of him. Myron had always been beautiful to him, but right now, he was like a dream, like someone from a different realm. Otherworldly gorgeous and captivating, as if he'd put a spell on Abel, making it impossible for him to look away.

He mentally went through the lineup of the Kraken, Seattle's hockey team, then ran through old playbooks from college, anything to prevent himself from coming. He was so hard, so fucking close. His body shook with it, demanding that Abel release the tight hold he had on it, but he dug deeper. He'd promised Myron he wouldn't let him down, and he wouldn't.

He put his hands on Myron's hips, loving the contrast of Myron's pale skin with his own bigger and much darker hands. The next time Myron came down, he helped him, pushing him down, hard even, as he drove his hips up.

"Oh fuck," Myron moaned. "Do that again."

He did, and he kept it up, resulting in a litany of sounds falling from Myron's lips. He was lost now, his eyes closed as he rode Abel's dick hard and fast, his hand moving in sync on his cock.

"Oh... Oh fuck...Yes!" he shouted and jerked as he spurted all over his hand, drops landing on Abel's stomach.

So. Fucking. Hot.

Abel waited until Myron's body had stopped shaking and his eyes had focused again. Then he snapped his hips and drove up inside him. He let go of the impossibly tight hold he had on himself, and with two more thrusts, he came. His orgasm slammed into him, detonating in his balls and launching up his cock. He shivered, jerked, shuddered, and twitched until finally his body signaled it was done.

"Holy shit," he rasped. "That was fucking amazing."

Myron winced as he climbed off him, his ass probably tender after that round. No wonder. He hadn't been gentle with himself. Again, it was Myron who cleaned Abel, efficient and quick, and he watched him through heavy-lidded eyes.

For a moment, he feared Myron would kick him out again, but then Myron crawled back onto the bed. Abel lifted his arm, and Myron snuggled close, draping himself half over Abel. "Thank you," he whispered after what had to be five minutes of silence, though it had felt comfortable to Abel.

"For what? I'd say we shared the pleasure equally."

"No, not that. For letting me be in charge. Again."

Oh, that. "It's important to you."

He said it as a statement, not a question, but Myron still answered him. "It does. I've had..."

He stopped talking, and his body tensed.

"You don't need to explain," Abel said. "I'm okay with it."

"Why? Most men aren't that easy in surrendering control."

"I don't care. Control isn't important to me, not in my personal life and not in bed. In my job, yes, but outside of that, I couldn't give two shits."

Myron was quiet for a long time. "I need control in every area. I didn't have it growing up, and I've had some bad experiences with hookups, so I can't let someone else be in charge anymore."

Abel's heart ached for him. "I'm sorry. But it doesn't matter to me."

He all but held his breath, though he forced himself to stay relaxed. Would Myron bolt again or kick Abel out? Would even the suggestion of more encounters between them send him running again?

"I don't do relationships," Myron said.

"Okay," Abel said easily.

"So if we keep doing this, it doesn't mean anything."

"Understood."

"I'm serious. I don't want to be tied down and end up unhappy in some horrific marriage."

Wow, what the hell had happened to him that he was convinced that was the only possible outcome? Not something Abel would bring up now, but he filed it away. "You set the pace. I told you you're in charge. We don't do anything you don't want."

Another long pause. "Okay."

Abel held him closer, his heart almost bursting with happiness. He had him. All he had to do was go slow and show Myron how good they would be together, how beautiful and amazing love could be. He'd work hard every day to gain his trust...and someday Myron would love him back.

12

I t had started with Abel staying over again one night when the weather had turned nasty and Myron felt bad about sending him home at one in the morning, especially since they both had to work the next day. And because he didn't have a spare bedroom, they had spent the night cuddled up in Myron's queen bed. Abel was like a fucking furnace, and halfway through the night, Myron had given up on the idea of staying under the covers and instead had kicked them off and sought his warmth from his lover.

Then Abel had left a toothbrush in the bathroom, saying he wanted to be able to brush his teeth. Reasonable request, right? The same was true for some spare clothes, in case he spilled something or got dirty or wet from the weather. Myron had cleared a shelf in his closet for him, surprised to find it almost full three weeks later. When had that happened?

When he was grocery shopping now, he automatically bought Abel's favorite microbrew, made sure he had a supply of the disgustingly sweet French vanilla creamer Abel loved in his coffee, and always had the peanut butter-filled pretzels the man was addicted to. And Abel rarely went home anymore but instead spent most of his nights at Myron's. And he didn't mind it as much as he'd thought.

They watched TV. *Inkmasters* had been the most logical choice, of course, but they also watched other reality shows and documentaries, and they discovered a mutual love for British detective series. And they had dinner together almost every night, hung out on the couch, and had sex on every surface in the house.

Spectacular sex, with Abel happily bottoming for Myron. He'd never asked to top again, and Myron wasn't sure if that was because he didn't want to or because he was afraid to suggest it. He'd have to bring it up sometime because as much as he loved to top, he definitely wanted to ride that fat cock again. That had been epic.

"You're whistling," Hao said at the end of the day after the last customer had left. They managed to make it sound like an accusation, which was quite the feat.

"Yeah, so?" Myron snapped.

"Dude, you don't whistle. Ever," Mari chimed in. "It's disturbing."

"I'm happy-ish, okay? So sue me."

Mari leaned on the halfway between their booths. "Let me guess. It has something to do with Abel DiRossi."

Hao fanned themselves. "That man is whew, so hawt..."

Myron busied himself with cleaning his tattoo chair. "It's just sex."

"Sure it is, honey." Myron didn't need to look at Mari to know she was rolling her eyes at him.

Myron snapped off his gloves and dumped them in the trash together with the paper towels he'd used to clean. "Look, I made it crystal clear that I'm not interested in anything more, okay? If he chooses to believe in a happily ever after for us, there's little I can do to stop him. He's a grown-ass man."

Mari's eyes softened. "So it wouldn't bother you if he broke things off and went searching for someone who did want something more serious?"

Myron froze. "What do you mean? Did he say anything? Did you see him with someone else?"

"For fuck's sake, Myron, that man is besotted." Hao slammed the drawer shut. "Get your head out of your ass and recognize what's right in front of you before you lose it."

Lose it? Was he at risk of losing Abel? A flare of panic shot through him, his heart clenching so painfully he gasped. What if Mari and Hao were right? What if Abel did grow tired of waiting for Myron and broke things off and chose someone who was willing to commit?

It shouldn't matter. Hadn't he assured himself almost every day that it was just casual and temporary? Then why did it hurt so much to imagine being on his own again without Abel? His bed would be so cold, his house so empty, and his heart...

His heart would be broken.

Oh god, he'd fallen in love with him. How the fuck had that happened? He'd been so determined to keep his emotional distance, yet somewhere along the way, he'd lost his heart anyway. Now what? What did he do now that he had realized he never wanted to let Abel go again?

The very thing that had seemed so impossible for him, so unattainable, was now within reach. All he had to do was tell Abel. Abel loved him. He hadn't said those words exactly, but that was probably more to avoid scaring off Myron. But Myron had seen it in his eyes, and the man showed it in everything he did every day.

Yes, Abel loved him, and he loved Abel, but he had to do

more than tell him. He had to show him, give him something for his patience, his selflessness as he waited for him. He needed to make a gesture that would speak louder than words.

And then the idea popped into his head so clearly he gasped all over again. That was it. Before he could talk himself out of it, he texted Abel.

Meet me at my shop at 6.30 for your tattoo. I have a design.

"What are you up to?" Hao studied Myron. "You look like a cat who ate the canary."

Myron took a deep breath, nerves already thundering through his body, even though he still had two hours. "You were right. I needed to recognize what was right in front of me...and I have a plan to do just that."

Hao's face broke open in a wide smile. "Good. I knew you were smart enough not to let that man go."

Between clients, Myron worked on his design for Abel. He found some sketches online and used them as inspiration to make his own drawing on his iPad. He tweaked and twiddled with it until he was convinced it was perfect, then transferred it onto a stencil. He'd eyeballed the size, having a reasonably good idea of the size of Abel's ass cheek, but he'd have to test it to make sure.

And then he waited.

13

Myron had a design for his tattoo? Abel didn't know what to think of that. They hadn't even discussed it after the first few times, and while Abel hadn't forgotten about it, he'd thought Myron had. Clearly, he'd been wrong, though his text had come out of nowhere.

What had he come up with and why now? Abel's gut told him something had happened, but no matter how much he went over everything that had passed between them in the previous days, he couldn't come up with anything that stood out. He'd have to wait and see and, in the meantime, trust Myron to do right by him.

When he arrived at Rainbow Ink, Myron was the only one left, setting up his booth. Abel knocked on the front door, which was closed, and Myron hurried over to let him in.

"Hi." Myron sounded breathless, his voice higher pitched than usual.

"Hey."

Abel hesitated, then leaned in and kissed him the same way he always did when he came home. He took his time, the kiss grounding him, steadying him. Whatever was happening, things felt good between them, so he'd trust that.

"Do you trust me?" Myron asked as if reading his mind.

Abel nodded. "I do."

"I don't want to show you the design before I put it on."

"Okay."

"Yeah? You trust me that much?"

"I'd trust you with my life, so my ass isn't a problem. You've certainly taken good care of it so far." He winked at Myron and got a cheeky, relieved grin in return.

"True. Okay, on your stomach, then."

Abel took a few steadying breaths as he stripped off his pants while Myron closed the front door again and pulled the curtains shut like they always did at night. The tattoo table was cold to his naked skin, and Abel shivered as he positioned himself facedown, his bare ass on display.

He closed his eyes as Myron began, not saying a word as he shaved him thoroughly. Just his right ass cheek, though, but maybe he had a design that would require multiple sessions? Myron dried his skin, cleaned it, and put a stencil on it. "Ah, perfect. My estimation of the dimensions was spot on."

Abel smiled. "I would've been surprised if you hadn't known the size of my ass by now, considering how much time you've spent inside it over the last few weeks."

"True, but fucking and inking are two different things."

He had a point there. Abel stayed quiet as Myron went through all the steps Abel had performed thousands of times himself. Transferring the stencil onto his skin.

Changing gloves. Selecting a needle. Ointment. Ink. And then the buzzing began, and the needle hit his skin.

Myron didn't speak as he worked. Abel sank deep into his thoughts and hovered in that pleasant state between being asleep and awake, his thoughts aimlessly drifting as he was happily relaxed, the endorphins of the tattoo coursing through his body. He didn't even try to determine what Myron was creating. He'd see it when Myron had finished.

He had no idea how much time had passed when the buzzing stopped and he returned to reality. Myron cleaned the area he'd worked on. "Yeah." His voice was hoarse. "That's exactly how I pictured it."

Abel's stomach fluttered with nerves as Myron helped him up, holding him as he got used to being vertical again before he led him to the tall mirror. Abel turned sideways, his eyes zeroing in on his ass.

He gasped.

A tattoo of a horse, meticulously done in fine lines, adorned his right ass cheek. It was beautiful. Stunning. Myron had captured the animal so perfectly, every line powerful.

Then the meaning sank in. "Myron..." he whispered and looked from the mirror to Myron, who studied him with wary eyes, as if he wasn't certain how Abel would react.

"It's me," Myron said hoarsely. "The wild horse is me."

He'd inked the animal with its head held high, tension in its body, and yet it wasn't resisting the rope around its neck. It was allowing itself to be caught, to be led.

Abel turned around and faced him. "It's perfect...and so are you."

"I'm scared. I'm not good at this, at being soft and social and thinking of someone else instead of just me. But for you, I want to try. You make me want to...be caught. I think..." He bit his lip, and Abel had never loved him more. "I think you'd be careful with me, that you'd tame me without breaking my spirit."

"Always," Abel swore. "I'll never force you to do anything you don't want to."

Myron stepped closer, wrapped his arms around Abel's chest, and rested his head against Abel's shoulder. "Could you please tell me you love me?"

Abel smiled, his heart all soft and fluttery at the wonder of holding his man in his arms and having permission to not only show him how he felt but tell him as well. "I love you so damn much. You have my heart. You've had it from the moment we met, and I promise I will love you till the day I die."

Myron sighed, his warm breath dancing over Abel's skin. "Doesn't it scare you to feel that way about me? As if I hold your happiness in my hands and could break it with one careless word?"

"My love isn't that fragile, and you're not that cruel. But yes, it is scary, but I think it's supposed to be. All the good things in life are. Without risks and fear, we'd never step out of our comfort zone."

"Mmm." Myron was quiet for a long time. "You have my heart as well. I don't know when I lost it, but it's yours. I'm... I love you, Abel. Just please, be careful with me. I'm not as strong as you."

Abel pulled him closer, his heart dancing in his chest. "I'll treasure you, my wild stallion. You were born to be free, and I promise I'll always respect that."

"Okay. In that case, I think I would very much like to be with you. Like, permanently."

Abel closed his eyes, the surge of emotions inside him so

strong he had trouble keeping himself from crying. "I would very much like that too."

The End

ARE you curious what happened to Reid, Myron's boss, and the wedding his sister broke off? Read his story in Jilted: Jaren!

BOOKS BY NORA PHOENIX

If you loved *Marked*, I have great news for you because I have a LOT of books for you to discover! Most of my books are available in audio as well trough Audible and iTunes.

The Foster Brothers

Growing up in foster care, four boys made a choice to become brothers. Now adults, nothing can come between them...not even when they find love. The Foster Brothers is a contemporary MM romance series with found family, sweet romance, high heat, and a dash of kink.

Forty-seven Duology

The Forty-Seven Duology is an emotional daddy kink duology with a younger Daddy and an older boy. Also includes first time gay, loads of hurt/comfort, and best friend's father.

White House Men Series

The White House Men series is an exciting romantic suspense series set in the White House. The perfect combination of sweet and sexy romance, a dash of kink, and a suspense plot that will have you on the edge of your seat. Make sure to read in order. Seven books in total. The series is complete.

Perfect Hands Series

Raw, emotional, both sweet and sexy, with a focus on Daddy kink, that's the Perfect Hands series. All books can be read as standalones. Five books. The series is complete.

No Shame Series

If you love super steamy MM romance with a little twist, you'll love the No Shame series. Sexy, emotional, lots of kink, with a bit of suspense and all the feels. Make sure to read in order, as this is a series with a continuing storyline. Five books. The series is complete.

No Regrets Series

Sexy, kinky, emotional, with a touch of suspense, the No Regrets series is a spin off from the No Shame series that can be read on its own. One book out with more to come.

Irresistible Omegas Series

The Irresistible Omegas series is an mpreg series with all the heat, epic world building, poly romances (the first two books are MMMM and the rest of the series is MMM), a bit of suspense, and characters that will stay with you for a long time. This is a continuing series, so read in order. Ten books. The series is complete.

Irresistible Dragons Series

The Irresistible Dragons series is a spin off from the Irresistible Omegas series described above. It has dragon shifters, wolf shifters, mpeg, suspense, and all the feels. Three books out with more to come.

Ballsy Boys Series

Sexy porn stars looking for real love, that's what the Ballsy Boys series is about. Expect plenty of steam, but all the feels as well. They can be read as standalones, but are more fun when read in order. Five books. The series is complete.

Ignite Series

The Ignite Series is an epic dystopian sci-fi trilogy where three men have to not only escape a government that wants to jail them for being gay but aliens as well. Slow burn MMM romance. Series is complete.

Stand Alones

I also have a few stand alones, so check these out!

- **Professor Daddy** (sexy daddy kink between a college prof and his student. Age gap, no ABDL)
- **Out to Win** (two men meet at a TV singing contest)
- **Captain Silver Fox** (falling for the boss on a cruise ship)
- **Coming Out on Top** (snowed in, age gap, size difference, and a bossy twink)
- **Ranger** (veteran suffering from PTSD falls for a sunshine animal trainer, cowritten with K.M. Neuhold)
- **Every Shade** (collection of shorts and novellas)

MORE ABOUT NORA PHOENIX

Would you like the long or the short version of my bio?

The short? You got it.

I write steamy gay romance books and I love it. I also love reading books. Books are everything.

How was that?

A little more detail? Gotcha.

I started writing my first stories when I was a teen...on a freaking typewriter. I still have these, and they're adorably romantic. And bad, haha. Fear of failing kept me from following my dream to become a romance author, so you can imagine how proud and ecstatic I am that I finally overcame my fears and self doubt and did it. I adore my genre because I love writing and reading about flawed, strong men who are just a tad broken..but find their happy ever after anyway.

My favorite books to read are pretty much all MM/gay romances as long as it has a happy end. Kink is a plus... Aside from that, I also read a lot of nonfiction and not just books on writing. Popular psychology is a favorite topic of mine and so are self help and sociology.

Hobbies? Ain't nobody got time for that. Just kidding. I love traveling, spending time near the ocean, and hiking. But I love books more.

Come hang out with me in my Facebook Group Nora's Nook where I share previews, sneak peeks, freebies, fun stuff, and much more: https://www.facebook.com/groups/norasnook/

My weekly newsletter not only gives you updates, exclusive content, and all the inside news on what I'm working on, but also lists the best new releases, 99c deals, and freebies in gay romance for that weekend. Load up your Kindle for less money! Sign up here: http://www.noraphoenix.com/newsletter/

You can also stalk me on Twitter: @NoraFromBHR

On Instagram:

https://www.instagram.com/nora.phoenix/

On Bookbub:

https://www.bookbub.com/profile/nora-phoenix

Printed in Poland
by Amazon Fulfillment
Poland Sp. z o.o., Wrocław

21304338R00045